FERGUS
and
MARIGOLD

For Chloe

Designed by Paul Cooper Design

Printed and bound by Proost, Belgium
for the publishers Piccadilly Press Ltd,
5 Castle Road, London NW1 8PR

A catalogue record for this book is available from the British Library

ISBNs: 1 85340 478 0 paperback
1 85340 413 6 hardback

Tony Maddox lives in Droitwich, Worcestershire. Piccadilly publish his wonderfully successful FERGUS series: FERGUS THE FARMYARD DOG, FERGUS'S UPSIDE-DOWN DAY and FERGUS'S BIG SPLASH. They also publish his SPIKE books: SPIKE THE SPARROW WHO COULDN'T SING and SPIKE'S BEST NEST.

FERGUS THE FARMYARD DOG   FERGUS'S BIG SPLASH   FERGUS'S UPSIDE-DOWN DAY
ISBN: 1 85340 174 9   ISBN: 1 85340 388 1   1 85340 284 2

SPIKE, THE SPARROW WHO COULDN'T SING!   SPIKE'S BEST NEST
1 85340 196 X   ISBN: 1 85340 466 7

FERGUS
and
MARIGOLD

Tony Maddox

Piccadilly Press • London

Fergus wasn't pleased.
He had been looking forward
to having a nice lazy day.
But Mrs Coddle had brought
her cat Marigold to stay at the
farm for the day.
"Humph!" he thought grumpily.
"Cats are trouble!"

"I'll find somewhere quiet," thought Fergus, "where that cat won't bother me."

So he went to the big barn.

In the yard, Marigold was up to mischief.
She jumped out at the hens
and gave them a scare.
"Cluck, Cluck, Cluck!" they squawked.

She crept up behind the ducks
and chased them into the duck-pond.

"Quack, Quack, Quack!" they protested.

She even surprised the pigs
by pulling their curly tails.
"Oink, Oink, Oink!" they cried
crossly.

Clucking, quacking and oinking,
the animals rushed into the big barn
to hide from Marigold.
Fergus groaned.
"Some lazy day this is!" he thought.
"I'll have to find somewhere else to sleep."

When he looked out of the barn
he saw Marigold prowling around,
looking for more mischief.
"Woof, Woof!" he barked in warning.
The animals scrambled to find places
to hide.
"I'm off!" thought Fergus.

He hurried across the yard towards
the washing hanging on the line.
A sudden gust of wind blew one of the
sheets which wrapped itself round him.

He yelped in surprise and
tried to get free.
Marigold turned to see
a scary white flapping thing
making the strangest yowling noise.
"Meeow!" she shrieked in fright.

She ran out of the yard, into
the orchard and up the nearest
apple-tree.

When Fergus told the animals
where Marigold was, they came
to see for themselves.

She stayed up the apple-tree
until Farmer Bob climbed up
his ladder and carried her down.
"I think the animals must
have scared her!"
said Farmer Bob's wife.

"Humph!" said Fergus.